This book belongs to

. . . .

ISBN 978-1-338-22880-9

10 9 8 7 6 5 4 3 2 1   18 19 20 21 22

Printed in China   62

First printing 2018

www.peppapig.com

Book design by Jessica Meltzer

When I Grow Up

Story adapted by Marilyn Easton

SCHOLASTIC INC.

Today in school, Madame Gazelle asks the children
what they would like to be when they grow up.

When I
Grow Up

She has a basket full of fun hats for them to choose from. The children are so excited to dress up! They run to the basket and each grab their items.

"Madame Gazelle, I don't know what I want to be when I grow up," Peppa says.

"Don't worry, Peppa. You have plenty of time to think about it," Madame Gazelle replies. "You can use the costumes to help you decide!"

Rebecca Rabbit knows what she wants to be when she grows up. She wants to be a queen. Queens get to wear crowns and tell others what to do!

Emily Elephant wants to be a teacher.

"Wonderful!" says Madame Gazelle. "Teachers are very important. What is it about being a teacher that you like the most, Emily?"

"Teachers get to be in charge!" Emily replies.

"I see . . ." says Madame Gazelle.

"I want to be a police officer when I grow up," says Freddy Fox. "The police drive cars with flashing lights and sirens!"

"Me too!" says Wendy Wolf. She is dressed as a sheriff. A sheriff is a kind of police officer who is in charge of all the other police officers.

"Thank you, Freddy and Wendy. What else do you like about being a police officer?" asks Madame Gazelle.

"They tell others what to do!" reply Freddy and Wendy.

Next it was Suzy Sheep's turn to share. "I would like
to be a doctor or a nurse," says Suzy Sheep.
"How lovely. Why do you think you would like that
job, Suzy?" asks Madame Gazelle.
"Because they help someone who is sick to get better.
And they tell others what to do," Suzy Sheep says.

Madame Gazelle explains to her students that jobs are about more than being in charge. Some jobs, like a doctor or a teacher, are about helping others. Some jobs are about creating something new, like a builder or an artist.

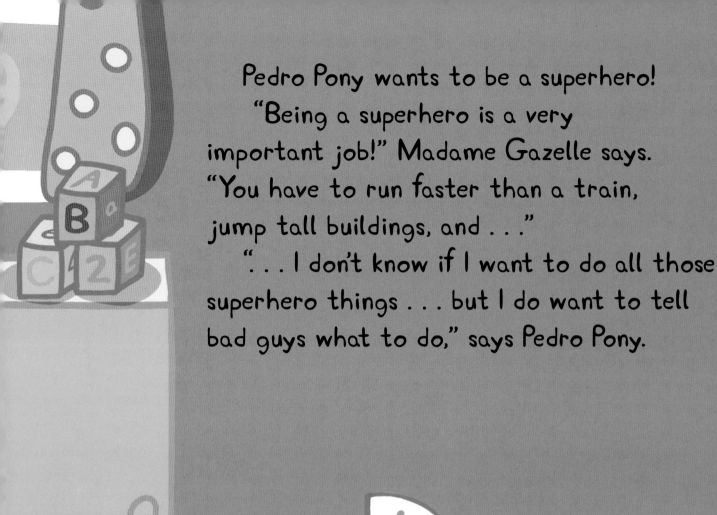

Pedro Pony wants to be a superhero!
"Being a superhero is a very
important job!" Madame Gazelle says.
"You have to run faster than a train,
jump tall buildings, and . . ."
". . . I don't know if I want to do all those
superhero things . . . but I do want to tell
bad guys what to do," says Pedro Pony.

On the way home from
school, Peppa tells Mummy Pig about
her day.

"So tell me, what did you learn today?"
Mummy Pig asks.

"Madame Gazelle asked us what we
want to be when we grow up,"
says Peppa.

"That sounds nice," says Mummy Pig.
"Not really, Mummy! Everybody knows what they want to be, but I don't!"

"George, do you know what you want to be when you grow up?" Mummy Pig asks.

"Dine-saw!" cheers George.

"You see!" says Peppa.
"Don't worry, Peppa. You have plenty of time to decide what you want to be!" Mummy Pig replies.

"What do you do, Mummy?" asks Peppa.
"I work on my computer," Mummy Pig answers.

"Do you get to tell others what to do?" Peppa asks.
"No, I don't," replies Mummy Pig.
"Well, that's no good then!" says Peppa.

Soon, Daddy Pig comes home from work.
"What is your job, Daddy?" asks Peppa.

"I could tell you, Peppa, but I think you'd find it a bit boring," replies Daddy Pig.

"I wouldn't, Daddy! Please tell me! Pleeease!" says Peppa. *Snort!*

"Well, Peppa, I work in a big office and help plan big, important buildings," Daddy Pig explains. "And I get to carry a briefcase and wear a suit!"

"Do you like your job, Daddy?" Peppa asks.
"I like it, but not everyone would," Daddy Pig
explains. "Everyone is different, Peppa."

That night, Peppa is still thinking.

"What can I do when I grow up?" asks Peppa.

"Think of something you like doing all the time," says Daddy Pig.

"I like jumping up and down in muddy puddles!" Peppa says.

"Well, Peppa, there aren't many jobs with puddle jumping . . ." Daddy Pig explains.

"But I am *very* good at puddle jumping!" Peppa says.

"Yes, I suppose you are!" Daddy Pig agrees.

"When I grow up, I will show everyone in the world how to jump in muddy puddles!"
"That sounds like a very good idea," says Daddy Pig as he shuts off the light.

Soon, Peppa and George fall asleep to sweet dreams about dinosaurs and puddle jumping.